# THE GHOSTLY SOLDIER

# THE GHOSTLY SOLDIER

Edgar J. Hyde

CCP

First published 1998
Reprinted 1999 (twice)

Text supplied by Joseph Boyle



ISBN 1-902012-17-8

Printed and bound in the UK

# Contents

# Chapter 1

"Hurry up children, keep up," shouted Mrs Martin trying to keep the whole class together. "Come on you two, we don't want to lose you," she added, glaring at Angus and Ishbel who had fallen further behind the rest.

They were staring at a small stone pile. Mrs Martin had called it a "cairn". In the middle of the cairn there was a smooth flat piece of stone with the word "MacLeod" inscribed on it.

The two children were still imagining the

scenes of over two hundred years ago when almost the whole MacLeod clan had been killed at the battle of Culloden. Mrs Martin had just been telling them some of the stories about the battle.

As Angus looked around, he could see the many cairns that had been erected all over the field where the battle had taken place, commemorating all the other clans who had fought at the battle. Angus looked over to the far side of the field. In the distance he could make out the large white flag that marked the spot where the English army of redcoats had lined up on the morning of battle. He closed his eyes and tried to picture the scene. He imagined he was standing in the middle of the Scottish clans, in his kilt, covered in mud from sleeping rough the night before. He had his claymore in one hand and his dirk in the other. He imagined the noises and the smells of the battlefield and tried to sense the feelings that a young Scots soldier would have felt that morning. Mrs Martin had described it as a mixture of fear and excitement.

Oh, how much Angus would have loved to be there on that morning in April. He had been brought up on the history and stories of Culloden and indeed the age-old struggle between the Scots and English. Ever since his family had moved to a small village very close to the battle site, he had been enthralled by the stories of bravery, gallantry, mystery and romance that had gone hand in hand with Scots history itself. Even though he knew well that the Battle of Culloden had been a disaster for the Scots army and it's leader, Bonnie Prince Charlie, Angus would have given anything to line up with the clans gathered that day to fight off the English army. He even dreamed that, somehow, he would have made a difference, carrying out some amazing feat of bravery that would have turned the tide of battle in the Scots favour and brought about a famous and historic Scottish victory. He would have stood proudly beside his King, the rightful King of his country, his claymore sword held high.

He opened his eyes again and glared at the flag in the distance. That was where the Duke of Cumberland had stood and ordered his English army to advance. That was where he had stood when he had ordered his army to put every Scottish male to the sword, even the helpless and injured. He had not been called "The Butcher" for nothing.

"Come on, Angus. We had better catch up!" Ishbel shouted trying to stir her brother from his daydream.

"Look, the others are way ahead. Come on, hurry up," she added.

Angus looked over to his sister and smiled.

## *Chapter 1*

"Don't worry, Sis. They won't leave without us," Angus replied, turning away from the battlefield and starting up the path that led back to the Visitor Centre.

Angus and Ishbel were 14-year-old twins and in the same class. Although they looked a lot alike, they were very different. Angus was very excitable and full of beans, constantly on the go. He was also a dreamer, and loved imagining himself in all sorts of adventures. Ishbel on the other hand was more composed and controlled. Her natural intelligence was supplemented by good common sense – something her brother had a significant shortage of. She shared her brother's love of Scottish history, but she had a more balanced view of her country's past, recognising the tragedy as well as the glory. She knew well all the stories of glorious defeat that her brother seemed to forget too easily. They both loved to visit the battlefield. It was very close to their village and their school often came on trips there to teach not only about the famous battle that had taken place, but also to teach about their ancestors' way of life.

"So which clan were you fighting for today, Angus?" Ishbel asked, only half mocking her brother and his daydreams. She knew what he had been imagining. It was always the same with him.

"Does it matter, Sis? We still won!" Angus replied, pretending to thrust his imaginary claymore towards her.

"Won? How would you know? You would have run a mile, and when the "Butcher" caught you, you would have been mincemeat, Scottish mincemeat!" Ishbel scorned, pushing her brother's outstretched arm away.

"Catch me? He would never have caught *me*. His overweight redcoats would have been no match for this speedy warrior!" Angus stated, stopping in his tracks, and then darting from side to side as if to emphasise how illusive he could be.

"Well let's see how speedy a warrior you are then. Race you to the Centre!" Ishbel challenged, stealing a good start on her brother who was too busy avoiding redcoats.

"You cheat!" exclaimed Angus, as he started after his sister.

But it was too late. She had made a good ten yards on him already, and she was hard enough to beat from an equal start.

The two arrived at the Centre a few seconds apart, gasping for breath and just in time to hear Mrs Martin announcing that the bus was ready to leave.

"See, Sis, told you they wouldn't leave without us," Angus stated, ignoring his recent defeat, and smiling towards Ishbel.

"Come on, let's go, Angus. We'll come back and see off the redcoats another day."

Angus looked back towards the flags in the distance and the old battlefield. The sound of the piper on the Centre steps added to the atmosphere of the place. Angus's mind was tempted to wander again.

"OK, Sis, I get the window seat this time," demanded Angus, running on, making sure he got the head start this time.

"Some warrior!" Ishbel thought, watching her brother weave through the people ahead.

## Chapter 2

"Hi kids, how was your trip?" Mrs MacDonald asked, hearing the twins rushing though the front door.

"Great, Mum. Did you know that Jimmy MacLeod's great, great, great, great, great grandfather fought at Culloden?" Angus stated, still filled with excitement from the day's trip, throwing his bag on the kitchen table.

"Who told you that, Angus? Jimmy, I imagine!" asked Mrs MacDonald, smirking. "I know Jimmy's dad, and if his ancestors are anything like his dad, the only fighting they would have done would have been at the local public house – or inn, I suppose it was then – on a Friday night!"

"He did, Mum, honest! We even saw the MacLeod Cairn." Angus pleaded, not recognising his mum's teasing.

"Cairn? Jimmy's dad probably built that one night to impress his drinking pals!" Mrs MacDonald continued, teasing her son.

"Och, Mum!" Angus exclaimed, eventually realising his mum was joking.

Ishbel shook her head. Her brother was so gullible.

"On you go you two. Get your homework done. Dinner will be ready in an hour or so," Mrs MacDonald ordered, her tone changing. Family routine demanded homework to be done before anything else.

"Is Dad home yet?" Angus asked, looking to find his dad's car in the driveway.

"He's in the garage working on his car. That old thing's falling to bits. The exhaust fell off today. It's an embarrassment," Mrs MacDonald replied.

"No, Mum, it's a *classic*," Ishbel stated, mocking her dad's continued belief that the 35-year-old vehicle he had owned since his teenage days was worth holding on to.

"Come on, Angus, maths tonight. I'm sure you'll be able to get the hang of the three times table soon!" Ishbel teased.

"Ha, ha, Einstein. Let's go," Angus replied, dragging his sister by the arm and heading up the stairs.

Eventually the noise from the two larking about died down, and Mrs MacDonald was satisfied that the homework was under way.

The evening passed quickly with Mr MacDonald only appearing briefly to eat his dinner. He spent the rest of the time hidden away in the garage trying to breathe new life into his beloved car.

The twins had spent the time after dinner watching television, in between occasional bouts of good-hearted teasing. Finally Mrs MacDonald announced that it was time for bed.

"Go out and say goodnight to your dad, you two. And tell him to come in – he has been out there all night. Tell him there's a cup of tea ready. That should bring him running," Mrs MacDonald said, switching the television off and heading for the kitchen.

Angus and Ishbel extracted themselves from the couch and started towards the garage, which stood to the side of their house. The garage was another piece of Mr MacDonald's handiwork. He had built it himself shortly after they had bought the house.

## *Chapter 2*

As the twins went out the front door and turned towards the garage, a strange blue light confronted them. Everything in front of them was lit up by the pale blue light. They looked at each other, a little bit confused by the sight of their "blue" front garden. From round the corner of the house they could hear a loud hissing noise. Both the noise and the light were clearly coming from the garage.

"What's going on?" Angus quizzed, expecting his sister to have a reasonable answer to hand.

"Don't ask me," replied Ishbel, taking her brother's arm.

Angus realised that this was one of those times when he should act the man and take control of the situation. However his wobbly knees were making it difficult to move. He composed himself.

"Come on. Nobody from Mars has been

here in a while. It's probably just a police car taken a wrong turn!"

Ishbel appreciated her brother's sense of humour but could tell that he was confused and a little apprehensive also.

Angus took his sister's arm and walked slowly forward to the corner of the house. The two stopped and looked at each other. The question of who was going to go round the corner first was clearly in their eyes. Angus's apparent warriorlike courage of earlier in the day was a distant memory. Ishbel was his older sister after all. A whole two minutes older.

"On you go then," Angus insisted, pushing his sister's arm forward.

Ishbel shook her head, "Some clan chieftain you would make!" she replied scornfully.

Ishbel put her hand on the corner of the house and edged forward. She moved her head slowly, getting ready to peer quickly round the corner. She could feel her brother tight behind her, his breathing quick and short. Ishbel's head started to clear the corner. She had her eyes closed, too afraid to look.

"What do you see?" demanded Angus.

Ishbel opened her eyes.

"Oh my God!" she screamed. In front of her, clouded in the blue light, was a strange being in what looked like an astronaut's suit. Or that was what she thought she saw. She didn't have the chance to look further. Angus had been startled by Ishbel's scream and in an effort to push himself away, had thrown Ishbel to the ground. Her leg had caught his and Angus too went tumbling – the two falling into a heap on the driveway a couple of yards in front of the garage.

"What are you two up to?" Mr MacDonald shouted, pulling the protective guard up and over his head, the acetylene torch still hissing away with its blue flame in his other hand.

Ishbel and Angus looked at each other and started to laugh. It was a nervous, relieved laugh.

"Just come to say goodnight, Dad," they both said in unison.

"What are you doing Dad?" Angus asked, trying to recover his composure.

"Just trying to weld some of this old beauty's bits together, son. My mate, Jim loaned me this oxyacetylene kit for a couple of days. It's working wonders," Mr MacDonald replied, turning the valve on the large gas tank off and hanging up the blow torch.

"Come on, it's late, let's get you two to bed," Mr MacDonald added, pulling the garage door down and turning the key in the lock.

Within minutes, Angus and Ishbel were

in their rooms, tucked up in bed. They both lay under their covers, smiling at their own stupidity. With the sounds of their parents chatting downstairs, they quickly fell asleep.

Angus had no idea how long he had been sleeping. He didn't know what had caused him to wake up. At first he didn't notice the strange orange glow that entered his room through the small gap in his curtains. Angus's room was at the side of the house and his bedroom window looked down on the top of the garage.

Gradually Angus came too. He looked around his room, the orange glow fooling him that it was morning time. Angus looked at his watch. It was only two o'clock in the morning. Angus couldn't believe it. What was going on? He sat up in bed and reached for the curtains.

The bright orange flames were almost reaching Angus's windowsills. The garage was on fire! The flames were already breaking through the garage's wooden roof. This time Angus acted without hesitation. He ran to his parents' room and within seconds his dad was on his feet and ordering everyone to get out of the house.

Within a few minutes they all stood in the street outside the house and a small crowd had quickly gathered. It hadn't taken long for the neighbours to notice what was going on. The crowd was made up of both those concerned and those just plain nosy.

As the fire engines arrived, the garage was completely engulfed in flame. There was a real danger that the flames were going to cause the MacDonald's house to catch fire also. Just as the firemen were jumping down from the engine and starting to get their equipment out, there was an almighty explosion that shook the whole street and a single ball of fire leapt high into the night sky through the roof of the garage. The firemen hesitated, waiting to see if any further explosions would take place.

The chief fire officer was deep in conversation with Mr MacDonald. The explosion was likely to have been the gas tank Mr MacDonald had been using earlier. The firemen then acted quickly and, within seconds, it seemed the flames had been reduced to small flashes. Ten minutes later, the firemen were starting to put their equipment away, hundreds of gallons of water having reduced the burning garage to a soggy, smouldering mess.

Angus was amazed at how quickly it was all over. Their house was safe. Angus looked towards his mother and sister, standing a few yards away. They were tight in each other's arms, his mother's earlier panic having passed now that she knew her family and her house were safe. Her eyes were still full of tears, still somewhat shocked by the events of the last half hour or so.

The crowd began to drift away and, within an hour or so, Angus and Ishbel were back in bed. This time they were in one of their neighbours' houses. They had not been allowed to go back into their own house for safety reasons.

As Angus drifted off to sleep, he was sure he could hear music – the faint strain of bagpipes – but his eyes were heavy and he had experienced too much excitement for one day. He quickly fell asleep.

# Chapter 3

A few days had passed since the garage had gone up in flames. After his family's nerves had returned to normal, Mr MacDonald's thoughts had been preoccupied by the loss of his beloved car. Mrs MacDonald, while at the same time terrorised by the experience, was delighted that the old "heap" was now gone and the family could at last be seen driving about in something, at least considered, normal.

The fire investigators had confirmed that the fire had probably been caused by a leak in the gas tank. The tank had probably fallen over and caused a spark that would then have set the leaking gas alight. They had all been very lucky. Angus had been hailed as a hero. The chief fire officer had said that if he hadn't raised the alarm sooner then the MacDonald house would have almost definitely gone up in flames too. The family's lives would have been in real danger then.

Mrs MacDonald had banned her husband from all DIY activities for the time being. Mr MacDonald, feeling rather sheepish about the whole episode, was happy to comply.

Angus was not slow to overplay the hero and his sister didn't like having to put up with his parading and glory seeking. However, secretly she was proud of Angus's quick action – she just wasn't going to let him know about it. His head could hardly get through the front door as it was. He may not have saved Bonnie Prince Charlie at the battle of Culloden, but he had saved the MacDonald family.

For the time being every request of Angus's was being granted, every treat allowed. So much so, that when Angus had asked for a new tent, his dad had appeared that very same day, with the very latest model from the local camping shop. His dad had even agreed when Angus had asked if he and Ishbel could sleep out in the tent, overnight, for a few days.

It was now Friday and, as Angus and Ishbel left for school, Mr MacDonald promised to set up the tent that afternoon for them, so they could use it that night.

At school, Angus had of course embellished and exaggerated the garage story so much that even his friends were getting fed up with him. Although it had been big news the next day, after a few days the boys in

Angus's class had had enough. Angus had got the hint and had turned his thoughts to the next few days in the tent. He had loved the times that Dad had taken Angus and his sister camping in the hills near their village. Ishbel had hated it at first, but, after she had got used to all the strange noises that disturb the quiet country night, she too had begun to enjoy it.

When they met at lunchtime the twins started to plan the adventure of the next few nights, trying to draw up a list of the "goodies" they would take into the tent with them. Sandwiches, books, sweets, a torch, personal stereos etc. Although camping was supposed to be about experiencing the quiet, natural life, modern camping in Ishbel's mind allowed a few personal luxuries. That included a few of her favourite CDs.

"Just to drown out some of the night's noises," Ishbel had insisted when her brother had tried to ban the personal stereos from the list.

The two returned from school full of excitement and anticipation of the night ahead. It was the start of the school holidays. With their parents locked up in the house, they could get up to whatever they wanted. No lights-out deadline tonight. Mr MacDonald was busy clearing away the debris of the burnt-out garage, filling a large skip that had been delivered the day before. The twins ran past him, with the briefest of acknowledgements, to the back garden to see if the tent was up.

There it was! A large blue construction with an orange weather sheet over the top and eight long guy ropes stretching out, anchoring the tent firmly to the ground. The twins dived through the entry flap and started wrestling about inside.

"Calm down you two. You'll bring the

whole thing down on top of you!" Mr MacDonald shouted, coming through to the back garden. He thrust his head through the open flap.

"Well, what do you think then? Happy?" he asked.

"Great, Dad – thanks very much," Angus replied rubbing his hand through his dad's hair, messing it up.

"Superb, Dad," added Ishbel, leaning over and kissing her dad on the cheek.

Mr MacDonald pulled his head back, stood up and started back towards the house.

"Well, that's those two taken care of. Now how to get on the right side of the wife?" he thought as he entered the kitchen through the back door.

Mrs MacDonald was still making him suffer for almost burning the house down. She had been frustrated by his DIY efforts for years. Many had been disasters, but this latest episode had topped the lot. It would take him a while to get out of the dog house on this one. Well, he'd start by cooking the dinner tonight and, with the kids out of the house, maybe he would be able to appease her with some flowers and a bottle of wine, he thought optimistically.

Meanwhile, Angus and Ishbel had calmed down in the tent and started to plan the evening ahead. Ishbel had dancing lessons to go to first and Angus was meeting some of his pals down the park for a game of football. However as soon as dinner was over and it was starting to get dark, they agreed that it was time to take up residence in the tent. Angus had taken out a new book of ghost stories from the local library and was looking forward to trying to scare his sister witless. Ishbel on the other hand had bought a new CD at lunchtime and was looking forward to snuggling into her sleeping bag with a big bar of chocolate and her personal stereo. She only hoped that Angus wouldn't spend the whole night acting up.

At nine o'clock exactly, as Mr MacDonald headed to watch the news, Angus and Ishbel made their way down the stairs with all their "goodies" and headed for the back garden and the tent.

"Now, don't stay up all night!" Mrs MacDonald shouted from the front room.

"And, Angus, don't frighten your sister," Mr MacDonald added. "Your mum and I want a nice quiet night."

The twins didn't reply. Smiling at each other they opened the kitchen door and headed for the tent.

After an hour or so inside the tent, Angus's ghost stories weren't going down well and after scoffing several bars of various types of chocolates, the two settled down in their own corners of the tent – Ishbel to listen to her personal stereo, Angus to read his latest football magazine.

It was a dark but cloudless night and the garden was only barely lit by the two torchlight beams, from inside the tent.

Angus looked over to his sister. It was difficult to tell if she was awake or asleep as she lay with her eyes closed with only the hiss of the earphones breaking the silence in the tent.

Suddenly Angus sat up. He could hear another noise. At first he thought it was just a new track on whatever CD Ishbel was listening to. But as he listened, he knew that wasn't the case. At first he couldn't make out what the noise was. It was a constant, melodic, high-pitched drone. But as the noise got louder and louder, he began to recognise the unmistakable strains of bagpipes. Not one bagpipe, more like ten or twenty, in the distance, but getting closer all the time.

Angus shook his sister. "Ishbel, wake up. Listen, do you hear that?" Angus demanded, shaking his sister's shoulder.

Ishbel opened her eyes and pulled the earphones from her head. She had been sleeping.

"What is it Angus? I was fast asleep," Ishbel complained.

"Sshhh, listen. What can you hear?" Angus asked again

Ishbel turned her head to the side as if straining to hear.

"It's only bagpipes."

As soon as she had spoken she realised what she had just said. It was after ten o'clock at night. People shouldn't be out playing bagpipes at this time.

"What are you up to Angus? Is this one of your tricks?" Ishbel demanded, remembering that she had been asleep, allowing her brother to set up some practical joke. But there was a look in her brother's face that told her that this was no joke.

She didn't wait for his answer and started to untie the flap that led out to the garden. Her fingers fumbled with the knots.

As the last knot worked free, Ishbel poked her head through the gap and out of the tent.

"Angus, look at this," Ishbel said, her voice betraying her nervousness.

Angus pushed up next to his sister, the two of them on their knees, heads sticking out from the tent.

The scene outside the tent was like a foggy winter's night. The whole garden, in fact as far as they could see, was covered in a deep, grey, swirling mist. The bagpipe noise was getting ever-closer. The sound was becoming deafening as if they were right outside the tent. Ishbel and Angus looked at each other and wondered if it was all a dream. They could see nothing and yet, the noise was almost upon them. They were both now feeling very scared. They stared hard at the mist, trying to see through it, trying to make out what was going on.

And then, suddenly, within touching distance, the swirling kilts were clearly in sight, marching past the opening of the tent – almost as if they had marched right through the tent. Angus started to count . . . four . . . six . . . ten . . . twelve pairs of legs. The mist was so thick that it was impossible to see above their waists, but it was clear enough to recognise that twenty-four kilted pipers were marching right through their garden.

And then almost as suddenly as it had come, the noise of the bagpipes, and with it the sight of the pipers, disappeared into the night.

Ishbel and Angus didn't know what to say. Fear froze them to the spot. They couldn't believe what they had just seen. The fear that was holding them suddenly let go, and the two jumped to their feet and ran at top speed for the house – Angus's cry of "Help!" drowning out his sister's.

# Chapter 4

"Calm down, kids. Calm down!" Mr MacDonald insisted, trying to make sense of what the twins were shouting about.

So far he had understood, "mist", "bagpipes", "pipers", "disappeared", but none of it was making any sense. The twins had burst into the front room just as Mr MacDonald was beginning to snooze on the couch. His anger had quickly turned to concern as he could see that his children were clearly upset.

Ishbel was the first to pull herself together and tell her mum and dad exactly what had happened.

When she had finished talking, Mr MacDonald sat silently and looked at his two children with some bemusement. He then stood up and, followed by the whole family, walked silently to the back door leading out to the garden. He opened it and they all looked out. The large tent was clearly visible in the centre of the garden. There was no mist and there were certainly no pipers.

"Right kids. It's obviously been a bad dream," Mr MacDonald insisted, not realising that his two kids would have to have had exactly the same dream at exactly the same time.

"But—but—Dad—" started Angus.

Mr MacDonald didn't give him time to explain further.

"No buts Angus. Come on – upstairs both of you. And Angus, give me that ghost story book. We've all had enough frights for one night."

Mr MacDonald closed the back door and ushered everyone inside. His anger had returned and the twins could see it would be useless to argue further.

As the twins made their way upstairs, Mr MacDonald turned to his wife.

"What a week – as if we hadn't had enough excitement!" he said

"Don't be hard on them dear, you know their imagination," Mrs MacDonald commented. "They're only young."

"I'd expect it from Angus – but Ishbel?" Mr MacDonald added. "Come on, it's been a rough week. Let's all get to bed."

Upstairs, the twins peered out of Ishbel's window. They knew what they had seen and they knew that it hadn't been a dream, but they couldn't understand it. Pipers in the mist! No wonder their dad had mocked them. It was ridiculous!

"What are we going to do about this?" Ishbel asked, still staring down at the tent below.

"There's nothing else for it. We'll have to stay in the tent tomorrow night and see what happens," Angus replied, lying back on the bed and trying to imagine what they could do to make his parents believe them. Perhaps it *had* been a dream, he thought.

"But what will we do if we see the pipers again?" Ishbel continued

"We'll deal with that when it happens. Maybe we'll never see them again. Let's not worry about that now. Come on, let's get some sleep." Angus replied, standing up and moving towards the bedroom door. "Don't worry, Sis, we'll sort this mystery out," Angus smiled as he went out the door. He wished he had a plan. But he hadn't.

# Chapter 5

The next day passed slowly. Angus and Ishbel just moped around, finding it difficult to concentrate. Although they tried not to think of the night ahead, it was impossible.

Angus played for his football team, who lost, and Ishbel went shopping with her mother and didn't buy anything. Angus's losing wasn't strange, but Ishbel not buying anything, now that *was* strange.

Eventually dinner passed, and after

watching some TV, the twins started to make for the tent.

"Are you two sure you want to stay out there tonight?" Mrs MacDonald asked.

"Don't worry, Mum. No dramas tonight, I promise," replied Angus, not sure if that was what he wanted or not.

"None of those silly ghost stories, Angus. Let's have a quiet night tonight, son, after the week we have had."

"OK, Dad, I promise," Angus replied, leaving the front room.

As the twins made their way across the back garden, Angus stopped and looked around. Again it was a clear, cloudless evening. It was just beginning to get dark and there was certainly no sign of mist or fog.

"Take note, Ishbel. No clouds, fog or mist in sight!" stated Angus, as if to record formally that it was a clear night.

## Chapter 5

When they were inside the tent they were unsure what exactly to do. Angus tried to crack some jokes, but neither he nor Ishbel were really in the mood. After fifteen to twenty minutes the two fell silent and lay back in their sleeping bags, listening to the noises outside. Ishbel started to remember her early days of camping again and began to feel bothered once more by every sound and movement outside. She was tempted to put her personal stereo on, but was afraid she would miss the possibility of hearing the noises that Angus had heard first the night before. She looked over at Angus. He seemed to be simply staring at the tent roof, waiting.

It was unclear who heard the noises first this time. They seemed to both sit up, alarmed, at exactly the same time.

"Here we go, Ishbel," Angus whispered, looking over at his sister, his voice a mixture of excitement and fear. He remembered the way his teacher had described the feelings of the young men on the Culloden battlefield. He knew now what she had meant.

The twins sat quietly, listening hard. As before, the melody started quietly. Gradually getting louder and louder. Angus quickly popped his head out of the tent and, just as quickly, drew it back in.

"All foggy again, I can hardly see anything." He confirmed what they had both expected. The strange mist had returned.

They waited till the sounds of the bagpipes felt as though they were right outside their tent, and when the music was right on top of them, they quickly thrust their heads outside the tent.

At first they could see nothing through the murky fog, that seemed even thicker than the night before. Angus thrust his arm out to touch the mist, almost as if to prove it was real. The ends of his fingers became invisible as they were devoured and disappeared in the magical mist. Just as he was about to pull his arm back in, Angus felt something touch his hand. It was the rough feel of a highland kilt.

And then they were upon them, once again, the army of pipers. Their legs appearing from either side of the tent and marching out and away from them. The noise from their bagpipes deafening.

Before Ishbel had a chance to react, Angus jumped up and pushed himself out of the tent. His sister tried to grab him, shouting.

"Angus! Stop – don't!"

But it was too late, he was gone. His whole body disappeared instantly into the mist as he ran forward. Ishbel's eyes darted from side to side trying to catch some glimpse of her brother.

She cried out, "Angus . . . Angus . . . don't leave me!"

But it was all in vain. Angus was gone. As the sounds of the pipers disappeared, and with it the mist, Ishbel was left alone in the tent, surrounded by silence. The silence was gradually broken by the sound of her own sobbing.

Angus couldn't believe his eyes as he rushed forward into the lines of pipers. The mist had disappeared instantly and he was now standing among the ranks of a full Highland piper line. He had to jump from side to side, avoiding the pipers trampling him down.

As he dodged the army of legs confronting him, he saw behind them another large number of men, in Highland battle dress, all rushing forward, screaming, with their swords waving high above their heads. Angus turned round. Ahead of the pipers and charging clansmen was a small line of men, dressed in the Redcoat uniform, that distinguished them as English soldiers.

"Oh my God!" thought Angus, his mind racing. "What on earth has happened? Where am I?"

Angus looked back and forth trying to make some sense of what had happened to him and where he was. But he didn't have time to think. He was immediately startled by the sound of a bullet whizzing past his head and shattering a boulder in front of him. Angus realised he had to move. He was in danger of either being shot or trampled to death. Either way he had to get out of there.

He looked around and saw a large rock about twenty yards away to his right. He ran off, diving behind the rock just as the kilted Highlanders came running past, their screams creating a scene of absolute terror. Angus waited for a few seconds, cowering behind the rock. Summoning up the courage, he lifted his head above the rock and stared at the events unfolding before him.

The group of Highlanders had reached the line of Redcoats and the scene was a mass of fighting bodies. Angus noticed that the distance between the rock and the battle was strewn with fallen pipers. A few pipers were getting to their feet and trying to re-start their pipes with whatever breath they had left in them.

The battle scene itself had disintegrated into a large number of individual skir-mishes, one man against another; Scottish claymore against English sabre. The screams were no longer screams of terror, but screams of pain. Men were falling all over the place, blood flowing from their fatal wounds.

## *Chapter 5*

Angus couldn't believe his eyes. He searched for the safety of his garden, his tent, and his sister. But it was useless, somehow he had been carried away from there to this horrible site. He felt nothing but terror. He buried his head in his hands.

However, Angus had no time to feel sorry for himself. As he knelt cowering behind the rock, his head in his hands, he felt a boot bury itself deep in his side, the pain shooting through his body.

"Ah . . . hah. Look what I have here. A young, scared one. You deserve to die, you Scottish coward."

Angus looked up and saw the bearded soldier standing over him. His red coat dark in patches with the blood of his enemies. The soldier grinned. Angus was frozen to the spot, his whole side and back still aching from the blow he had received.

"Well, my little warrior, let's hear you

squeal. This is for all my dead mates!" The soldier snarled.

Angus watched as the Redcoat lifted his rifle high above his head. The dagger bayonet at the end of the rifle glinted in the moonlight. Still grinning, the Redcoat started to thrust the rifle down on the helpless youth. Angus closed his eyes and screamed. He felt the weight come down upon him. But instead of the sharp pain he expected, it was a colossal thud. He opened his eyes. Lying across his body with his head right next to Angus's, was the English soldier. He was dead. His eyes were still open and his face was frozen into the same evil grin.

Angus looked up. Standing high on top of the rock was a young Highlander, muddied and covered in blood. His claymore dripping red from its most recent blow.

"Well, that's at least the hundredth time I've seen him off," the young Highlander exclaimed, wiping his claymore on the dead soldier's coat. "That Corporal Campbell takes some killing!" he added a broad smile lighting up his face, the whites of his eyes and his teeth contrasting with the dirt on his face.

Angus didn't know what to think. But the sense of relief he felt was overpowering. Although he was confused, he knew that he had been close to disaster, close to death. He wasn't sure if he was safe yet.

The highlander kicked the Redcoat's body to the side allowing Angus to stand up. No easy feat as Angus's legs felt like pieces of elastic. He wavered and grabbed at the rock for support.

"Och, Angus, let me help you. I'm Jamie MacLeod," the young warrior said grabbing Angus and steadying him. "Let's get you home."

# Chapter 6

Ishbel sat back on her knees, the tears rising in her eyes. She was so scared. She had just seen her brother disappear in front of her very eyes. But before she had even a chance to work out what she was going to do next, or how she was going to explain her brother's disappearance to her parents, the entry flap in the tent started to move. Ishbel jumped to the back of the tent in shock.

Angus's head appeared in the gap.

"Oh, Angus, thank God you're safe!" Ishbel exclaimed, shuffling to the front of the tent, and reaching to embrace her brother.

But as Angus came through the flap, Ishbel noticed another figure following her brother into the tent. She looked again at her brother and noticed his face was ashen white. He looked as though he had seen a ghost. She turned quickly back to the strange figure that was now almost through the flap and into the tent. Ishbel knew that this was no one she recognised. Having seen the look on Angus's face, and the sight of this unknown stranger, Ishbel's initial relief was beginning to turn to concern. She began to wonder what had taken place in those few seconds that her brother had disappeared. The stranger was now fully inside the tent but didn't speak. As the tent flap fell shut, Ishbel glanced outside. The mist had returned. Ishbel started to feel scared again.

Ishbel turned to her brother who had huddled himself into a far corner of the tent with a sleeping bag wrapped around him, his face full of shock.

"Angus, what's going on? What happened? Where did you get to?" Ishbel asked, her voice both nervous and concerned, her eyes darting between her brother and the stranger.

Angus didn't reply. He looked up at his sister and simply shook his head, appearing confused.

"Angus, say something!" Ishbel exclaimed, beginning to get angry.

"Hush, Ishbel, be gentle with your brother," the stranger spoke quietly. "He has had a bit of a fright, poor lad."

Ishbel turned to the stranger. She looked at him. In the dimly lit tent it was difficult to make out his features. But the stranger's voice seemed friendly and without threat. She noticed now for the first time how he was dressed. He looked like someone from all the old drawings and paintings she had seen of the Scots of two hundred or so years ago. Dirty cotton shirt with plaid sash running from his shoulder to his waist. A rough woollen kilt, green in colour mainly, with a broad leather belt around the waist. On his feet were worn leather sandals. Ishbel, for some reason, noticed he had no socks, and the dirt on his feet and toes seemed like an inch thick. Tucked into his black belt he had a large sword and beside it a small dagger.

Ishbel summoned up all the courage in her body.

"And who are you?" she managed to splutter out before her courage disappeared.

"Me? I'm Jamie MacLeod. Best fighter in the MacLeod clan," the stranger stated boldly, straightening his body up as if to emphasise the point. A broad smile lit up his face.

Ishbel peered at him through the darkness. Somehow she didn't feel threatened by him. Her fear began to subside.

"He's just saved my life."

Ishbel turned to see her brother sit up, his face beginning to look something nearer normal.

"You wouldn't believe what I have just seen, Ishbel," Angus continued.

"Well somebody had better tell me what the heck is going on before I bail out of here and take refuge in my bedroom," Ishbel demanded impatiently.

Her common sense told her that there must be a rational explanation for all these strange goings on.

"Listen, Ishbel, and for once don't interrupt," Angus insisted, his composure returning.

Angus went on to tell her all he had seen, and all that had happened from the moment he stepped into the mist. The pipers, the screaming clansmen, the Redcoats, and the battle that followed. Ishbel listened without interrupting – too astonished to say a word. If it hadn't been for the stranger sitting opposite she would have thumped him on the head and told him to stop wasting her time.

Jamie's presence was a physical testament to everything her brother was telling her. When Angus reached the part in his story where his death seemed inevitable, Ishbel's face started to turn the colour her brother's had been moments earlier. Still, she didn't interrupt, concentrating like someone who is reading a book, desperate to find out the ending.

When Angus finished, everyone in the tent remained silent. Ishbel didn't know what to say.

"But . . . but . . . you disappeared for barely a few seconds," Ishbel managed to mutter.

## *Chapter 6*

"Time is nothing in my world," the stranger stated solemnly.

Angus was feeling a mixture of relief and yet also excitement as he began to realise what an adventure he had just been on.

"It was amazing, Ishbel, amazing," Angus said, shaking his head, still in some shock.

The kilted Highlander spoke up.

"Och, it wisny anything special. Ah get up tae that every night," he said, waving his arm as if to emphasise the insignificance of Angus's recent episode.

Now both Angus and Ishbel were staring at the young Highlander. Angus, now more composed, noticed that the stranger in front of him was probably not much older than he was. Two or three years at most.

"Jamie, who are you? What are you doing here, in our garden, in our tent?"

"Well, would you believe, my friends,

Ah've been here in your garden for over two hundred and fifty years, give or take a year or so," Jamie answered, his grin disappearing and a look of sadness coming over his face.

The twins remained silent, waiting for the young stranger to continue.

Jamie continued his story.

"I don't come from your time. I come from a time long since past. I was born in the year of Our Lord, seventeen hundred and thirty."

"But that's impossible..." Ishbel interrupted.

"Not impossible. Not impossible at all," Jamie replied, holding up his hand to stall any further interruptions. He continued.

"I am a member of the MacLeod clan. We lived on a small village on the shores of Loch Carron in the west. My father, uncles, cousins, and friends followed the standard of

Charles Stuart, the 'Bonnie Prince'. It was a noble cause. We had followed him to Derby in England and rejoiced as we watched the Redcoats scamper at our every advance. We were invincible. And then some cowardly lords persuaded him to turn back. We would be left at peace, they said. Pah! They hadn't counted on the 'Butcher'. He hounded us. Never allowed us to return peacefully. He followed our every move, harried us, chased us. Pushed us ever northwards till we had only the sea at our back. And there we fought and there we all died."

Jamie paused. His face tightened, the sparkle in his eyes faded. He lowered his head.

"So you were at Culloden?" Angus asked, excitedly, insensitive to the youth's obvious pain.

Jamie looked up. "We never made it to Culloden. The group we were with had separated from the main army, searching for food. The Prince had ordered it himself. The army had been marching for so long. We were about thirty in all. We had collected some grain, some barley and oats from local farms and were on our way back to join our comrades at Culloden. We knew Cumberland's men were close.

"It was my father who had spotted them first. A small group of Redcoats, a similar number to us, thirty, maybe forty. They were doing the same as us, collecting food. We had no choice. We had to fight through them to reach Culloden. It was useless. They were better armed than we were. We fought bravely. They fought bravely. To a man we fought to the death. Everyone died. Well almost everyone. As I lay in the mud with my own blood spilling from me, I looked into my father's eyes. I can remember his words 'Be brave son, MacLeod forever.'

## Chapter 6

"As my eyes closed for the last time in the real world I watched him disappear through the trees towards Culloden."

Angus and Ishbel stared at the young Highlander, lost for words. Jamie's head was lowered, his thoughts seemingly in another place. When he lifted his head his eyes were full of tears.

Jamie went on, "When Cumberland's army came upon us, after the big battle, sixty or seventy dead corpses, he simply ordered his men to bury us in the nearest ditch. No decent burial. Even his own dead soldiers were cast in with us, without Christian burial on sacred soil. No blessing. Nothing. We have never rested peacefully since. For almost two hundred years our troubled souls have risen and each night relive the day of our death, each man dying a thousand times over. Some years ago these houses were built over our heathen graves and our souls were locked in, here on your very land, still restless but unable to rise and fight our ancient battle. Suddenly, without warning, our souls were released again and our battle continues. It is our fate."

Angus remembered, immediately, his father's garage and the explosion that probably brought about this mysterious, ghostly release.

Ishbel sensed the sadness in the young clansman's words. She could see the sadness clearly written on his face. For Jamie, the glory and the adventure of battle had disappeared a long time ago. His was truly a troubled soul, living a real, and repeated, nightmare.

Jamie stood up and made to leave the tent. He turned to look at the twins, his face drawn and serious.

"Be careful. Never enter the mist. Me, I can die every night. You have still to meet your first death. Corporal Campbell and his mates will not spare you. Stay away from the mist."

With that, Jamie darted out of the tent and into the mist. Angus pushed the flap aside. He could just about hear the melodic strains of bagpipes in the distance. The mist cleared and the bagpipes were silent.

# Chapter 7

Angus and Ishbel sat silently in the tent, confused and frightened. Jamie had been gone a few minutes and yet neither had spoken. Both of them were almost too afraid to acknowledge what they had just seen and heard. To acknowledge that it were true, would mean that they were in the middle of something so strange, so weird, so fantastic. This was something that you only see in films, or read in books. Whatever it was, they both realised they were in the middle of something they couldn't handle on their own.

Ishbel started to move.

"Come on, Angus. We have to talk to Mum and Dad. We need help to sort this out."

"But they'll think we have gone crazy – completely loopy," insisted Angus, shaking his head.

"Well, we'll have to try and convince them. We can't have an ancient battle fought in our back garden every night," Ishbel said, her face breaking into a nervous smile. "What will the neighbours say?"

"Ha, ha, Ishbel. This is serious. If you had seen that Redcoat's face, and been staring up at that bayonet . . ." Angus started to reply.

"I know, I know. I'm only trying to control my nerves. Come on let's catch them before they go to bed," Ishbel interrupted, putting her arm around her brother.

"Right, that's it. The tent comes down tomorrow," Mr MacDonald snapped as soon as Angus and Ishbel had finished telling their story.

He had listened to their tale, with a smile on his face waiting for the punchline, waiting for one of them to let him in on the joke. When the twins had insisted over and over again, that it was no joke, his patience finally broke.

"Either you two are at it, or the books you are reading are filling your heads with such stories that you don't know when you are dreaming or not," he continued. "No more tents for you two!"

Ishbel and Angus continued to plead with their father. Eventually Ishbel came up with an idea.

"Dad. Maybe you are right. Maybe we

just have overactive imaginations. After all we were only at Culloden again the other day. But it would be a pity to get rid of the tent. Maybe we are still just a little bit too young to stay out on our own. Why don't you stay over in the tent with us tomorrow night. That way I'm sure we'll see that it was all just a bad dream," she said, putting on her most persuasive voice.

Mr MacDonald agreed readily. He hadn't wanted to get rid of the tent after all the money he had just spent on it. If he spent the night in the tent and nothing happened, no mist and no soldiers, it would sort the matter out once and for all.

"Right you're on. Tomorrow night it is. Now get up to bed before I skelp the pair of you!" Mr MacDonald said, raising his arm and aiming it at Angus's backside. The pretend blow never landed as the twins scampered up the stairs to the refuge of their bedrooms.

Angus thought Ishbel's idea was excellent. When his dad heard the bagpipes and saw the pipers, he would have to believe them. Then they could all start to work out what on earth they were going to do to sort it all out.

Ishbel and Angus spent most of the next day at the local library. They had decided to try to find out if there was any reference in the books in the library about the battle that Jamie had described in the tent the night before. He had said that it had taken place the day before the main battle of Culloden and their own house was only about three miles from the site of the famous battle.

But they searched in vain. They scanned through, what seemed like a hundred books looking for any detail or story that would have proved that what Jamie had described really happened. But they could find nothing. There was no reference in any of the books to a small battle taking place the day before the main battle. They returned home a little dejected but still with some excitement and apprehension for the evening ahead.

"Come on Dad, let's go," Ishbel said, trying to pull her dad up from the couch. Mr MacDonald's previous enthusiasm for Ishbel's idea had reduced somewhat. The thought of lying in a cold tent instead of his cosy bed was now not very appealing. He stood up, reluctantly, and grabbed the sleeping bag that Ishbel had dumped at his feet.

A few minutes later, the three of them were huddled together in their sleeping bags in the tent. Mr MacDonald's feeble attempts to imitate ghost noises had not impressed the twins and very soon the tent fell silent.

## *Chapter 7*

Angus and Ishbel lay motionless, trying to make sure that they did not miss the first sounds of the bagpipes. However, the first sounds that they heard where not the strains of the previous nights but the sounds of their dad snoring.

"Just leave him for now. We'll wake him when the pipers come," Ishbel whispered, leaning up on one elbow.

Angus nodded and lay back down. An hour or so passed without any strange recurrences of the previous night's events. Angus's eyes were beginning to feel heavy. He had begun to tire of concentrating on hearing every noise. Ishbel's slow deep breathing confirmed that she had already lost the battle against tiredness.

And then it started. At first Angus didn't move, wanting to be sure he wasn't mistaken. But as he listened and the music got louder, he knew that they were back. He moved to the flap and pushed it aside. The mist had returned also.

"Dad, Ishbel, wake up. They are here," Angus shouted, pulling at the sleeping bags.

Ishbel awoke immediately and rolled over to the entry flap. Mr MacDonald groaned and sat up, rubbing his eyes as he came out of his deep sleep.

"Angus, I'll kill you. What is it?" Mr MacDonald mumbled.

The noise from the bagpipes was now clear. Both Ishbel and Angus looked at their father waiting for the sleepiness to disappear and for the realisation of what was going on to appear on his face. But as they stared at him, his face remained blank.

"Dad?" Angus pleaded. "Can't you hear it?"

"Hear what?" Mr MacDonald quizzed, moving over to the front of the tent.

The music from the bagpipes was now

at its loudest. Angus pulled back the tent flap, the mist completely shrouding the garden.

"Look at the mist Dad. Look you'll see them any second," Ishbel added, sure her dad would see everything even if he didn't seem to hear the bagpipes.

"This is ridiculous. What mist? Look I can see the fence at the bottom, as clear as day!" Mr MacDonald snapped, grabbing his sleeping bag and heading for the flap.

"I'm off. You two, I want you in your own beds in two minutes, this nonsense has gone on too long."

Mr MacDonald stormed out of the tent into the mist just at the very moment the pipers' hazy images appeared marching past the tent. Angus remembered Jamie's warning about the mist as he watched his father disappear out of sight.

"Dad, don't! Come back!" Angus

shouted, scared that the mist would transport his father away as he had been the night before.

The flap fell shut. Both Jamie and Ishbel hesitated, as the sound of the pipers faded away and then disappeared completely. Ishbel pulled the flap open. The garden was clear and quiet. The mist had gone. The twins pushed their heads out of the tent, too afraid to speak. The night before, Angus had returned instantly from the mist, within seconds. They peered down the garden through the dim light.

"Right you two, what did I say? Get yourselves in here. NOW!"

Mr MacDonald was standing at the back door steps, looking back down towards the tent.

Angus and Ishbel looked at each other. It hadn't worked. Their dad had seen and heard nothing. Somehow all of these strange goings on were only visible to them.

If nobody else could see all of this, then they weren't going to get any help from anyone else. They were on their own.

# Chapter 8

That night, lying in bed, Angus's mind was racing. He had tried to convince himself time and time again that somehow, he and Ishbel were imagining all this. Surely, if it had been real, his dad would have seen or heard something. But each time as he recalled his encounter with Corporal Campbell and Jamie MacLeod he knew it had to have been real. He remembered, too vividly, the boot of the Redcoat digging into his ribs. His hand touched the spot where the boot had made contact. It was still tender and sore. That was real alright.

The next morning, just after they had all finished breakfast, the doorbell rang. Mrs MacDonald went to answer it.

"Angus it's for you, it's Jimmy looking for a game of football," Mrs MacDonald said, coming back into the kitchen.

Jimmy. Jimmy MacLeod. Angus smiled, and then the smile disappeared.

"Ishbel," Angus whispered not wanting to upset his parents again. "Ishbel, it's Jimmy MacLeod."

Ishbel looked at her brother, puzzled.

"Yeah? So?" she said.

"Remember what he said about his ancestor dying at the Battle of Culloden?" Angus continued, leaning low over the kitchen table.

Ishbel still looked puzzled.

"Jimmy MacLeod, Jamie MacLeod."

## Chapter 8

Angus repeated the names, allowing the connection to sink in with his sister.

"Jimmy MacLeod, Jamie MacLeod."

Ishbel hesitated, and then the penny dropped. She started to nod her head, seeming to agree with her brother's latest theory. And then almost as quickly her expression changed and she started to screw up her face.

"No way, Angus. No way. Jimmy MacLeod is always making up stories. There is no way he has anything to do with Jamie. It's ridiculous," Ishbel stated, keeping one eye on her parents who were at the far end of the kitchen, tidying up.

"It might be ridiculous, but it might not. Let's find out," Angus said standing up, heading for the hall.

Jimmy MacLeod was one of Angus's best pals from school. He was about six inches taller than Angus, although they were the same age. He was not the most clever of boys, but he was a real athlete. He was just about the best at everything the boys tried at school. As well as being tall, he was already well-built for his age. He was the best fighter at school, but the other boys had given up challenging him, knowing better now. Mrs Martin always referred to him as "The Big Highlander".

Jimmy's dad ran the local equipment hire company. It was Jimmy's dad who had loaned the oxyacetylene kit to Mr MacDonald to work on his car. That had caused some joking at school, the day after the garage had gone up in flames.

Jimmy was sitting on the stairs in the hall, throwing a football from hand to hand.

"Hi, Jimmy, let's go," Angus said, grabbing the ball in mid-flight.

Jimmy noticed that Ishbel was following behind her brother.

Jimmy frowned, "She's not playing football, is she?" he quizzed, looking somewhat disdainfully at Ishbel.

"No, no, Jimmy. Don't worry. We've just got something to tell you first. Come on let's go up to my room," Angus declared, grabbing Jimmy's arm and leading him up the stairs.

Angus looked down the stairs, making sure his parents were not hovering around, before he closed his bedroom door.

Angus started, "Jimmy, first of all you have to promise to repeat to no-one what we are about to tell you. Secondly do not interrupt until I have finished."

Jimmy looked puzzled but nodded his head. He liked a good mystery, and he was sure, from the serious expressions on the two facing him, that he was about to hear one.

Angus told the whole story, from the garage burning, right up to the night their dad had joined them in the tent. Ishbel interrupted only occasionally, her comments adding some weight to the tale.

Angus tried to make sure he missed nothing, not one detail. When he finished he sat back and smiled at Jimmy.

"Well, what do you make of it all?" he asked

Jimmy didn't know what to say.

He knew Angus was a bit of a joker, but Ishbel too? He had always regarded Ishbel as a serious level-headed girl. The fact that she was confirming everything Angus was saying made the strange tale just about believable.

Before Jimmy had a chance to say anything, Angus spoke again,

"Jimmy, the guy who saved my life, the one who came into our tent, his name was Jamie MacLeod, the same as yours. Jamie,

Jimmy, both forms of James. He could have been your ancestor."

Now Jimmy was beginning to become really excited. The thought of this mystery being linked to him and his family was more than a little appealing.

"Do you think so, Angus? Do you think he could really be my ancestor?" Jimmy asked, the excitement in his face evident.

Ishbel spoke up.

"Well, Jimmy, what do you know about this relative of yours who died at Culloden? Is it true? Who told you about it? Did he really die there? What was his name?" Ishbel fired the questions at Jimmy, demanding immediate answers.

But Jimmy's expression changed. His head dropped, and he stared at the floor. Angus was beginning to think that Jimmy had made up the story of his ancestor at Culloden.

Jimmy started to speak, "To be honest, I really don't know anything about it. I just remember when I was a kid my grandfather used to tell me all these stories about the old days. I don't know if any of them were true or not. I have forgotten most of them, but I always remember he told me to be proud of our name, MacLeod. He used to always say to me, 'Be brave son, MacLeod forever.' "

Angus and Ishbel looked at each other. Angus smiled and nodded. Those words were the very same words Jamie had said that night in the tent. The words Jamie's father had used as he lay dying on the battlefield.

"Is your grandfather still alive, Jimmy?" Angus asked keenly.

Jimmy looked up, "Course he is, lives in the next village, he does," he said sharply.

"Well, Jimmy, I think we need to pay him

a visit. He may be the one person who will understand all this," Angus said.

"More importantly, he may be the one person who will be able to help us sort it all out," Ishbel added, standing up and heading for the door.

# Chapter 9

Jimmy's grandfather's house was only a short bus journey away. On the way, Jimmy had asked the twins to go over their story again and again, especially the part where Angus had gone into the mist and ended up in the middle of the battle. Jimmy would have loved to have been with Angus that night. The idea of fighting Redcoats appealed to him a lot. He was sure he would have been able to take care of himself. Corporal Campbell would have been no problem to him.

Angus just smiled at his friend. He knew now there was a big difference between playing at soldiers and being a soldier. There was no way he had wanted to run into any of those Redcoats again.

As the bus stopped, the three friends jumped off, Jimmy leading the way. Old Mr MacLeod's house was at the end of a small lane. It was the last in a row of small cottages.

Ishbel noticed that his garden had been well looked after. The grass was neat and the borders were covered with all sorts of pretty plants and flowers.

Jimmy rang the doorbell. There was no answer.

"He's probably round the back, working in the back garden," Jimmy declared, "Come on let's go round the side."

Jimmy was right. The old man was on his knees, trowel in hand working at the bottom of the garden. As he turned, hearing the noise of people arriving, his face lit up.

"Jamie, my boy, good to see you," he shouted, getting to his feet.

Angus noticed immediately that Jimmy's grandfather had used the more Scottish version of his friend's name. This was all looking very interesting.

"And who is this you have brought with you, son?" Mr MacLeod asked looking at Ishbel and Angus.

Jimmy introduced his two friends as he helped his grandfather sit down on the garden bench. He looked like a robust old man but his old bones had stiffened up from the hour or so he had spent working on his garden.

It didn't take long for Jimmy to get to the point of their visit.

"Gramps, we need to talk to you, we need your help," Jimmy said, sitting down on the grass at his grandfather's feet. Angus and Ishbel joined him.

Mr MacLeod looked at the serious faces staring at him. He wondered what major catastrophe had befallen these youngsters. Probably broken some neighbour's window and wanted to borrow money, before their parents found out, he thought. Kids these days got all worked up about the slightest thing.

"Go on then, what's it all about. Speak up. Hurry, I've got the bedding plants to water, yet," he said sharply, pretending to lose his patience.

Once again, Angus began his story. The old man listened intently, his face remaining blank, expressionless. Angus related all the events of the past few days, trying to make sure he missed nothing out. As he finished, Angus half expected the same reaction he had received from his dad. He was afraid the old man would just laugh, chase them away and tell them not be so daft.

But the old man did none of that. He stood up.

"Stay here a minute," he said and walked off into the house.

A minute or so later he reappeared, holding what looked to Angus like an old piece of cloth. The old man sat down again on the bench.

"Do you recognise this," he asked holding the cloth out in front of him.

Angus and Ishbel looked at it. It was a tattered piece of tartan cloth. It seemed very old. The pattern was very faded, but the lines of the tartan design could still be made out. The cloth was mainly green in colour with, red and white lines running through it.

Ishbel recognised it first. It was the very same pattern on Jamie's kilt the night in the tent.

"Was his kilt like this?" the old man asked.

Ishbel nodded her head. She looked up at the old man. His eyes were beginning to water. Ishbel wondered what it had meant.

Mr MacLeod was silent for a few moments. He was clearly a little emotional. He coughed a little and then started to speak.

"This piece of cloth has been handed down in my family from generation to generation. The design is the ancient MacLeod tartan. The modern MacLeod tartan is quite different. After the battle of Culloden when so many of our clan fell, the ancient tartan was set aside never to be used again, in honour of all those who died. It was felt that no one would ever be worthy enough to wear it again.

"The story of that time has been handed down from generation to generation. This is the only piece of cloth left. It was taken from the battlefield and handed to my, now let me work this out again . . . great, great, great, great grandfather. He was nine years old at the time, and he had just been told that his father and brother had died at the Great Battle. He had been too young to go with them. His father's body had been buried with the other clansmen on the field itself where they fell, but they never found his brother's body or that of many others who had left the village to go and fight with the Prince."

The old man stopped. His eyes, again, beginning to fill up. He looked hard at Angus and continued.

"I think you have found them son. I think you have solved a mystery that has been in my family for over two hundred years. The women who followed the army had searched for days, trying to pick out our clansmen and bury them properly, where they could be blessed and their souls despatched to heaven. But so many of our men and boys couldn't be found.

"I think you have found them now. I believe your Jamie MacLeod is one of our lost kinsmen, my ancient grandfather's brother."

Angus was disturbed by the old man's stare. He had wanted the old man to believe them but, somehow, knowing that it was all real was a little scary.

Angus had never believed in ghosts and here was an old man confirming that he had been sitting next to and talking to one a couple of days previous. In fact, confirming that his garden was overrun with them every night.

"But why could my dad see nothing?" Angus asked of the old man, still a little confused.

"Sometimes only the chosen get to see the afterlife son. Who knows why these souls reveal themselves and how they choose who to reveal themselves to. It's not uncommon for children to be able to see what adults cannot," Mr MacLeod answered, smiling a little reassuringly to Angus.

Ishbel spoke up next.

"But why are they not at rest like all the others?" she asked.

"The answer was in your story itself, girl, in Jamie's own words. They were buried were they lay, without a Christian burial, without a priest or blessing. The "Butcher" had no time for them. Their souls have been cast into the middle-life, between heaven and earth," Mr MacLeod replied.

His voice wavered when he considered the fate of his ancient clansmen.

"But we have to do something. We can't leave it all like this. There must be something that can be done," Ishbel continued. "We can't leave them, we have to help."

Ishbel started to cry. Finally the realisation of all that was happening was too much for her. This was really happening. It was really true.

"Now, now, dear. Come on up here," Mr MacLeod said quietly, pulling Ishbel up next to him on the bench, and putting his arm around her.

"Angus, son, you say that it was the explosion in your dad's garage that started all this off," Mr MacLeod asked, looking directly at Angus.

"Yes, sir, I think so," Angus replied

"Well that's where we will have to start then," the old man added.

The three friends looked at each other. "Start what?" Jimmy asked.

"Looking for bones," Mr MacLeod replied. "Looking for bones, hundreds of them."

# Chapter 10

The old man smiled as he looked at their puzzled expressions.

"I hope you lot are not squeamish, especially you lass, we have a big job to do," he stated, his smile disappearing from his face.

"What are you on about, Gramps?" Jimmy asked, wondering if his grandfather was making any sense.

"Listen to me, you lot. The only way we are going to put these souls to rest is by digging up their bones and moving them to sacred ground," Mr MacLeod replied, a little irritated by his grandson's questioning manner.

"But if the bones are there, couldn't we just get a priest to come and bless the ground?" Ishbel asked.

"Who else is going to believe this story of yours. If you can't get your own parents to believe you, how do you think a priest is going to react? I can see him now. 'Yes sure kids, let's go now, just let me get my holy water.' Pah! Don't be daft. It's up to us. We'll have to do it ourselves." Mr MacLeod replied, mocking Ishbel's suggestion.

"But how are we going to manage? There must be hundreds of bones to dig up. We have no equipment. How will we do it?" Angus asked.

"Leave that to me, lad. My son, Jamie here's father, has plenty of equipment. We'll just have to borrow a few things, won't we, Jamie," Mr MacLeod replied, running his hand through Jimmy's hair, messing it all up.

"But Gramps, you're too old, you can't . . . there's no way. . ." Jimmy stammered

"Hold your tongue, Jamie lad, I'm not too old yet. Whose business was it before your father's? Eh? I taught your old man everything he knows. Remember that!" Mr MacLeod replied, rebuking his grandson.

Angus and Ishbel smiled. The old man was not to be messed with. At last they had someone who was on their side. Angus liked the sound of the old man's plan. But it was a big task. They had a lot of work to do.

"We need a couple of hours on our own without your parents around. Is that possible?" Mr MacLeod asked, looking from Ishbel to Angus.

"They are going out for a meal tonight, around 7.00 pm. It's their anniversary,"

Ishbel replied, remembering hearing her mum booking the table the other day.

"Perfect!" Mr MacLeod exclaimed, "I'll be at your house by eight at the latest. Jimmy you come with me. I'll need your help to gather the gear and to show me the way," he added.

With that, the old man stood up and headed back into the house. Angus, Ishbel and Jimmy watched him as he strode off, the earlier signs of stiffness seeming to have disappeared.

"You'd better go after him, Jimmy," Angus suggested, "he looks in the mood for action!"

Jimmy smiled, nodded and followed his grandfather. Angus and Ishbel headed back towards the bus stop. They didn't have to wait long for the bus and were soon back at home. As they walked up the pathway leading to the front door, Angus glanced over to the area where the garage had stood. His dad had been working at clearing all the debris away. The explosion had caused something of a crater, resembling the after-effects of a mortar or missile landing at the side of their house.

Angus walked over to the crater. Ishbel followed him.

"Let's have a look," Angus suggested pulling at his sister's sleeve and jumping into the crater. Ishbel lost her balance and fell in after him. Unable to keep her feet she ended up flat on her back in the dirt. Angus laughed, "sorry, Sis" he said, trying to hold back the grin that was breaking out all over his face.

Ishbel didn't move, unimpressed by her brother or his apology. She looked up at him.

"Get me up!" she snapped.

Angus walked over to his sister and offered his hand. Ishbel lifted her left hand to grab her brother and pushed the other into the ground, intending to grab some dirt and throw it at him. She froze suddenly. Her hand had found something long and hard and she pulled it quickly through the loose dirt. She held it up in front of her. It was unmistakable. A long bone. A human bone.

"Angus!" Ishbel screamed, throwing the bone to the side and leaping out of the crater. "Let's get out of here."

Ishbel disappeared round the corner of the house. Angus looked down at the bone. He knelt down beside it and started clawing at the dirt with his hands. It didn't take him long to find another, and then another. Before long he had a small pile of bones. The ground was full of them. Mr MacLeod had been right. Angus decided it was best to wait for the old man before doing any more digging. Angus picked up the bones and carried them to the side of the house. He found an old blanket and covered the bones. They were safe there till later. He looked at his watch. One o'clock. It was going to be a long day waiting.

Apart from a brief visit downstairs for dinner, Angus and Ishbel spent the day in their rooms. Neither seemed to want to talk about the night ahead. Angus looked out all his books on Scottish history and started filling his head again with the tales of glorious battles, of clans and claymores, Redcoats and rifles. The sensation of fear from his escapade a couple of nights previous was beginning to fade.

Ishbel tried hard to avoid thinking of anything to do with Scottish history. She pulled out every CD she had and listened to them, two and three times over.

Eventually the twins heard their parents preparing to leave for the restaurant.

"Now, no nonsense you two. We will be

back by 11.00, and you had better be tucked up in bed," Mrs MacDonald stated as she put on her coat.

A few minutes later the taxi arrived and they were gone. Angus and Ishbel spent the next hour or so sitting on the back of the couch, alternating between staring out the window and staring at the clock.

7.30, 7.45, 8.00, 8.10. There was no sign of Jimmy or his grandfather.

Suddenly, the noise was deafening. Angus looked up the street. At the top end of their street, just turning in from the main road, was a large JCB. Sitting in the driver's compartment were Jimmy and, at the wheel, his grandfather.

"What in earth is that?" Ishbel asked, gaping out the window.

"It's a JCB, a digger, an earth mover," Angus replied jumping from the back of the couch and running to the front door.

# Chapter 10

The JCB pulled up at the MacDonald driveway and Mr MacLeod jumped out. He walked up to the crater and stared at it, shaking his head.

"Right grab some shovels and stand back till I tell you," Mr MacLeod ordered, pointing over towards the JCB. Angus walked over to the giant jagged bucket at the front of the huge digger. Inside the bucket were three shovels. Angus grabbed them and handed them out.

"I'll use the JCB bucket to loosen up the ground in the crater. When I'm done you jump in and start digging. Put all the bones you find at the side there," Mr MacLeod said, jumping back into the digger.

The huge machine moved up the driveway. It stopped in front of the crater. The bucket dropped to the ground, digging deep into the crater, lifting the dirt high and then dropping it again. Mr MacLeod did this a few times before giving the instructions for Jimmy, Ishbel and Angus to start digging.

Within minutes they had accumulated a large pile of bones. Five times, the JCB moved in and dug deep into the ground. After each time the three friends jumped in, searching for all the bones they could find. The pile to their side was now huge. Ishbel had started to count them but had given up long ago.

After about an hour, the three jumped out of the crater. For the last ten minutes or so they had not been able to find any more bones.

"That looks like that's it," declared Mr MacLeod, "I think we have got the lot."

Angus leaned on the side of the house and looked at the pile of bones.

"I hope we are doing the right thing, Mr MacLeod," Angus said, a little mournfully.

"Trust me, lad. This is for the best. Come on, now. We have to hurry before the neighbours start taking an interest in our bit of digging. You two start tidying up. Jamie, help me pile these bones into the digger's bucket," Mr MacLeod replied, trying to keep them all going.

A few minutes later, the digger's bucket was full of bones and the crater, and the area around, had been tidied up as much as possible.

Ishbel and Angus jumped up and joined Jimmy and his grandfather in the driver's compartment. It was a bit of a squeeze but they all made it in.

As the JCB rolled down the street, Ishbel was sure that every one of their neighbours would be watching out their windows. She did not dare look and kept her eyes fixed on the road ahead.

"Where now, Mr MacLeod?" Angus shouted above the noise of the digger's roaring engine.

"Where do you think, lad? To the graveyard of course, sacred ground. That should sort out everything," Mr MacLeod replied confidently.

The graveyard lay next to the church about a mile outside of the village. Thankfully they didn't pass too many people on the way. The few that they had, had given them very strange looks. The sight of a packed JCB, rolling through the village at 9.30 or so was not entirely common.

After what seemed like an eternity, the JCB turned into the graveyard. Angus immediately saw what had delayed Jimmy and his grandfather earlier. At the far end of the graveyard there was a huge pile of dirt and beside it a large hole had been dug. The JCB had obviously been busy here too.

As the huge digger approached the hole, the bucket in front of them started to rise. As the digger's wheels reached the edge of the hole, the bucket turned over and released its strange cargo. The bones tumbled into the hole. The digger moved back and then with its bucket lowered, started to push the pile of dirt into the hole and on top of the bones. Two minutes later, the hole was gone, completely filled. They all jumped down from the JCB and walked to the side of the freshly completed grave. They were all silent.

Finally Mr MacLeod spoke. His voice was calm

"These pour souls have been restless for hundreds of years. Let us hope that they now find peace. We have done a good thing here tonight. Let us all say a silent prayer for them."

Angus, together with the others, lowered his head and quietly offered a prayer.

Minutes later they were back in the JCB and heading for home. As Ishbel and Angus jumped out of the cab, Mr MacLeod shouted after them,

"Don't worry kids, everything will be all right now. Their souls will be at peace. Sleep well."

The JCB roared off. The street fell silent. Ishbel and Angus headed up the path and into the house.

Neither of them noticed the old blanket and the small pile underneath it as they went through the front door.

# Chapter 11

Angus woke up with a start. He wasn't sure what had caused him to remember. Surely they hadn't forgotten them, he thought. Surely Jimmy or Ishbel had seen the pile and added it to the others. He looked at his bedside clock: 3.00 am. He pulled on a pair of jeans and a sweatshirt and opened his door. He could hear his father's heavy breathing from his parents' room. He had still been awake when they had returned from the restaurant.

He made his way quietly down the stairs,

trying not to wake anyone. The noise of the key turning in the back door seemed deafening, but nobody stirred. Angus made his way out the back and round to the side of the house. Its shape was clear, even in the darkness. Angus walked up to the blanket and lifted it. The small pile was still there. They had forgotten them. Angus groaned. What we he do now. He couldn't make it to the graveyard at this time. He walked round to the back of the house again and sat down on the backdoor step. He put his head in his hands and started to think what he would do. Should he contact Mr MacLeod again in the morning, or just take the small pile himself to the grave.

As he sat there staring at the ground, he didn't notice the mist gathering around him. It was thin at first, but within seconds it had thickened up. As Angus looked up he couldn't believe his eyes. His garden had disappeared and he was back in the middle of the field. The battlefield of the other night. He looked around. It was different. It was silent. There was no sound of pipers, no screaming highlanders, no line of Redcoats. They had all gone.

Angus stood up and started to walk around, trying to break out of the spell that had brought him here, trying to return to his back garden. He found the rock he had hidden behind the other night. He jumped up on top of it, just as he had first seen Jamie MacLeod do, as he saved his life. He looked around. Nothing, no one.

And then, the shot rang out, the bullet shattering a piece of rock at Angus's toes. Angus looked to the right. In the distance he could see a single figure, a single red-coated figure. He was reloading. His must have been the bones under the blanket. Angus couldn't believe he had been so stupid.

He started to run. The second shot whizzed past Angus's ear, hitting the ground a few yards in front of him. Angus looked back. The Redcoat was running after him now. Angus ran as fast as he could, but he felt as though his legs were made of lead. He did not dare to look back again. He could see a small group of trees in front of him. He had to make it there. He might be able to lose him there, he thought. He could hear the sound of the Redcoat's steps gaining on him.

The trees didn't seem to be getting much closer and Angus was getting very tired. He could hardly catch his breath. He was dragging his legs now through the heavy heather. He looked back. The Redcoat was almost upon him and was starting to pull the sabre at his side out from his belt. Angus now recognised the grizzly features of his attacker. It was Corporal Campbell. As Angus was looking back he didn't notice the large branch that had fallen from the trees in front of him. As he turned to look forward again, it was too late. His leg thumped against the branch and Angus went flying forward, crashing to the ground at the edge of the trees. He spun round quickly onto his back, grabbing at the branch to use as a weapon to fend off the Corporal's imminent blow. He was no more than a few yards away now, and Angus could see the evil grin appearing on his face as he realised he had his prey at his mercy.

Angus shuffled backwards until his head was blocked by the first of the trees. He watched as the Redcoat ran the last few paces towards him.

Angus heard it before he saw it. The noise sounding a bit like an arrow released from a bow. The thud as it stabbed into the Redcoat's chest like the thud of a dart hitting a dartboard. The Redcoat stopped suddenly in his tracks, his hand reaching for the dagger that now stuck out from his chest, his face contorted with pain. The blood started to run through his fingers, the wound fatal, the weapon piercing his heart.

The Redcoat fell to the ground, dead at Angus's feet.

Angus rose to his feet and spun round. A face he knew well appeared from behind one of the trees. Jamie MacLeod. His broad smile was a welcome sight for Angus.

The young highlander came out from behind the tree and walked up to the speechless Angus. He put his hand on Angus's shoulder and laughed loudly.

"How could you have forgotten us, ye daft sassenach," Jamie exclaimed, shaking the youth's shoulder.

Jamie's face turned serious, his smile disappearing.

"You have done a fine thing, Angus. My

clansmen are at peace, thanks to you," Jamie said solemnly. And then the smile returned to his face, "But I could do with you finishing the job. It'd be safer for you to get rid of us too. The next time you come visiting, I may not win," he added.

Jamie walked past Angus leaned over, picked up the dead Redcoat and threw him over his shoulder. As he walked away, Angus watched them until the mist shrouded them and they disappeared.

The mist cleared and Angus looked around again. He was back in the middle of his garden.

# Epilogue

As Angus sat on the bus, no one could have guessed at the contents of the bag at his feet. Only Ishbel, who sat beside, him knew. She had wanted to come with him to finish the job they had started the night before.

As they got off the bus, Jimmy and his grandfather were waiting for them by the graveyard's gates.

The old man smiled. Angus had phoned Jimmy and told him about the bones they had forgotten the night before. The second meeting with Corporal Campbell had been as close a call as the first. Angus didn't want a third.

The small group of four walked to the far side of the graveyard, sharing the peace of the graveyard's silence. The dark patch of the fresh grave was clearly visible as they approached.

The old man handed Angus the shovel he had brought for him. Angus dug about three feet of soil out of the ground in front of him. The ground was soft from the previous night's work He picked up the bag and emptied its contents into the hole, and then quickly threw the soil back on top, patting the new pile with the back of the shovel.

He stood back and looked at Mr MacLeod.

The old man smiled again and said, "May they all rest in peace now."

Angus replied softly, "Amen. Amen to that."